ERMYNTRUDE
AND
ESMERALDA

ERMYNTRUDE
AND
ESMERALDA

Giles **LYTTON STRACHEY**, 1880-1932

Introduction by Michael Holroyd

ILLUSTRATED BY ERTÉ

𝔰𝔡

STEIN AND DAY/*Publishers*/New York

Library of Congress Catalog Card No. 76-84828

Originally appeared in PLAYBOY Magazine

Copyright © 1969 by Mrs. Alix Strachey

Illustrations copyright © 1969 by Anthony Blond Ltd.

Designed by Bernard Schleifer

Stein and Day/*Publishers*/7 East 48 Street, New York, N.Y. 10017

SBN 8128-1265-4

Printed in the United States of America

To H. L.

INTRODUCTION

"Will you believe me when I tell you that I have begun and got well under way with a new facétie?" Lytton Strachey wrote to the artist Henry Lamb on 18 February 1913. *Ermyntrude and Esmeralda*, as he later called this comedy, was finished the following month at his mother's house in Hampstead, 67 Belsize Park Gardens, and dedicated to Lamb, with whom he was then very much in love. "Don't I deserve at least a lead medal for this?" he asked Lamb. "I'm actually enjoying it; but I see all too clearly it's a mere putting off of the worst moment—but enough!"

The worst moment, which was frequently being put off, was his final committment to write "Cardinal Manning," the first of the four polemical essays that were to form his celebrated *Eminent Victorians*. Nothing, at first sight, could appear more different in tone and content from the Manning essay.

Ermyntrude and Esmeralda was written as an exchange of correspondence between two upper-class seventeen-year-old girls, who have pledged themselves to find out all they can about the manifold mysteries of sex, and report their discoveries to each other by letter. There are many private jokes and autobiographical fragments. Ermyntrude's London home is based on Lancaster Gate, the ugly and portentous building where Strachey had spent twenty-five years of his youth: "It chills me to go down the staircase, with the dreadful dome at the top, and as for the drawing-room it's so big and so gloomy that I feel creepy whenever I go into it." Esmeralda's home owes something to the succession of country houses that the Stracheys would rent each year for their summer holidays. She is, of course, a far less substantial character—her heart's in the right place, but she hasn't any head. Her loyalty to Strachey's Cambridge is simply flippant and visual: "He's only a young man from Oxford, so he can be safely disregarded, can't he? I don't believe Oxford's as good a place as Cambridge, and light blue is my favourite colour." But Ermyntrude has many observations that must have been only too familiar to Henry Lamb— the fetish for ears, for example: "And his ears, do they stick out?—but I don't suppose they can or he wouldn't be called handsome. If they don't, please pinch one of them from me, as a punishment for his bad behaviour." Such remarks have many counterparts in Strachey's own letters to Lamb, and the personal fantasy which he put into *Ermyntrude and Esmeralda* enabled him to give the story an extraordinarily authentic ring. It is not simply that many schoolgirls are curious about babies, sex, and love, but that their curiosity takes just the sort of physical form that Strachey expresses. He has caught the tone perfectly.

10

Strachey wrote *Ermyntrude and Esmeralda* not for immediate publication but for the enjoyment of his friends. When Lamb left him, and England, after the outbreak of war, Strachey sent it as a kind of engagement ring to Mark Gertler the artist who he thought might take Lamb's place in his affections. But the charming offer came to nothing. It was, of course, a facétie—a joke. But the term is misleading for those who do not appreciate the nature of Strachey's humour. Wit, irony, exaggeration, melodrama, these were his methods of expressing the truth—often a personal if not a literal truth. It is when he is not humorous that the reader should beware of taking him seriously. In *Ermyntrude and Esmeralda* he is extremely amusing, but behind the humour there is a serious purpose. By using nursery terms for the genitals, he makes all the more ludicrous society's standard reaction of horror to sex and to sexual deviation. Implicit throughout the lightly-written satire is a scathing criticism of the taboos under which he himself suffered and the repressive procedures that governed the upbringing of adolescents, especially young girls.

In spirit therefore *Ermyntrude and Esmeralda* is not so very different to *Eminent Victorians* after all. By its totally dissimilar method, it attacks many of the same Establishment hypocrisies. It has been compared to Laclos's *Les Liaisons Dangereuses* both by Gabriel Merle (who has translated it into French) and by David Garnett, to whom Strachey in his ex-

11

pressive falsetto read it one evening over Christmas 1914. For he was seeking more than mere enjoyment from his readers, he was seeking sexual enlightenment and toleration. So receptive was David Garnett to this message that, after hearing the story for the first time, he proclaimed himself to be there and then converted for the rest of his potent life into a *libertine*—"that is a man whose sexual life is free of the restraints imposed by religion and conventional morality."

MICHAEL HOLROYD

12

ERMYNTRUDE
AND
ESMERALDA

I

My dearest Ermyntrude,

    At last I have a moment to spare, and can sit down and begin to carry out my side of our promise. How delightful it is! To have you to write to, my dearest Ermyntrude—you who are so lovely, so charming, so beautiful, and so clever! Not that there is anything to write to you about. You will ask why, if that is so, I have only just managed to get hold of a spare moment. The truth is that a great deal is always going on here—a great deal of fuss and absurdity—but nothing that is of the slightest importance, or that I could possibly write to you about. As you know, however many people there may be in the house, and whatever they may be doing, nothing ever really can happen in the country. How should it?—with no parties, no plays, no concerts, no shops, no dances—but that is an exaggeration—there are dances—about two in a year—and there's to be one next month, at the Swinford's, and—what do you think?—I am going to it! Yes! It has been settled so. Mama at first said I wasn't to—although I'd danced all through the one we had here last winter—and had my hair up too; but she said that I wasn't out, and that I must wait till next year. But then yesterday at breakfast when it was mentioned again, Papa

suddenly put his head up from the newspaper and asked why I shouldn't go, and whether I wasn't seventeen, and whether that wasn't old enough, and whether—oh, all sorts of things—whether I wasn't a pretty enough girl, and silly jokes like that. And so it was arranged, and I'm to wear a white silk dress that Carrie's making for me, and my Neapolitan sash, and the tortoise-shell comb that Aunt Louise gave me on my last birthday. Won't it be fun? I can't help being rather excited about it, and the boys are so ridiculous—especially Godfrey—who says I'm already beginning to look like Lady Clara Vere de Vere, and this morning I caught the tutor, Mr. Mapleton, smiling at one of their jokes, but what does that matter? He's only a young man from Oxford, so he can be safely disregarded, can't he? I don't believe Oxford's as good a place as Cambridge, and light blue is my favourite colour. Which is your's? When I said that to Godfrey he span round on one toe, and wouldn't answer. He never will answer half the things I say. I suppose all boys are like that; but as you have no brothers you won't know.

But I've been forgetting all this time to tell you the most interesting thing in the world. Who do you think is staying with us? The Dean of Crowborough! And oh, my dear, he is the most charming, beautiful, clever man you can imagine. That sounds as if I meant to make out that he was like you—which would be very absurd, because of course he isn't in the least—for one thing he's quite old—about fifty,

I should think—and for another he's very polite. I don't mean that you're not polite, but he's so particularly so—so grave and courteous—almost severe at times, and yet you soon find that he's wonderfully kind, and most attentive. He reminds me of those lines in Tennyson—

> And in his dark blue eye austere
> A lighted welcome lurked and glowed.

except that his eyes are not dark blue but pale grey, but that doesn't matter. I simply adore him—almost as much as I adore you, my dearest Ermyntrude. Do you think it possible that—perhaps—I am in love with him? I sometimes think I must be. My heart beats when he comes into the room, and the other day when he picked up my handkerchief, which I'd dropped without noticing, and said "Yours I think, Miss Esmeralda?" in his lovely voice, I'm certain I blushed. Supposing I was in love with him, and supposing he asked me to marry him! Wouldn't that be enchanting? Which reminds me of that conversation of ours at the end of last term about love and marriage and how you have babies and all the rest of it, when we stayed up so long talking and made Miss Bushell so angry, and it was all so perfectly delightful. Well, have you found out any more about it? Do tell me, because I'm sure I don't know what to think, and you're so much cleverer than I am. Can you have babies without being in love, and can you

18

be in love without—but oh dear, the boys are calling me to come and play stump cricket this instant, and I can't put them off any longer so I must stop. Do write soon, my dearest Ermyntrude, about all your gay doings in London, to

Your ever most adoring
Esmeralda

P.S. We are to have charades this evening, and tomorrow General Marchmont is coming, which will be a great bore, as he will probably do nothing but talk to the Dean.

II

My dearest Esmeralda,

   I was very glad to get your letter. I think, although you live in the country, you have much more to write about than I have. Your idea of my "gay doings" is quite imaginary. I hardly ever see any one, except of course the eternal Miss Simpson with whom I spend (it seems to me) the whole of every day, sitting up here in this old dark school room, and only emerging for the family meals and the daily patrol in the Park. My mother is always out, and my father is always at the House of Commons, and as that makes up the household you see there's not much opening for gaiety. It chills me to go down the staircase, with the dreadful dome at the top, and as for the drawing room it's so big and so gloomy that I feel creepy whenever I go into it. You say that nothing ever happens with you; well, at least you have stump cricket and charades and Deans and tutors to amuse you. I have racked my brains, and really the only thing I can think of that has happened here since I came back is—guess!—prepare your mind for something amazing—we have got a new foot man. But please observe that the important point about this startling occurrence is—not that the footman is new, but that his name is. He is called

21

Henry, and the last four were called George. Well! isn't that a change? I've also noticed that his finger nails are rather cleaner than those of the last two Georges. But those are details. To have to say Henry instead of George when one wants some more bread —that is the epoch. So you see you've no right to pretend that you live in a desert. And (I think) you've even less right to pretend that you're in love with the Dean. How could anyone be in love with an old man of fifty with pale grey eyes, and I'm sure also with pale grey cheeks hanging in folds, and one of those horrid necks that have a flap of skin in the middle? The truth is I believe you're shamming a romance with the Dean in order to conceal one with Mr. Mapleton. It's very suspicious. You say hardly anything about him. What is he like? Is he tall or short? Dark or fair? Is he good looking? According as you answer these questions I shall judge. So take care. I have forgotten whether Godfrey is the brother who is a year younger than you or another. Please tell me what he looks like too. Has he got brown curly hair and large dark eyes in your style, I wonder?

I've tried to go on with our enquiries about love and babies, but I haven't got much further. The other day I began edging round the conversation in that direction with old Simpson, and naturally that didn't succeed. She shut me up when I was still miles off. Everyone always does—that is, everyone who knows. What can it mean. It is very odd. Why

on earth should there be a secret about what happens when people have babies? I suppose it must be something appallingly shocking, but then, if it is, how can so many people bear to have them? Of course I'm quite sure it's got something to do with those absurd little things that men have in statues hanging between their legs, and that we haven't. And I'm also sure that it's got something to do with the thing between our legs that I always call my Pussy. I believe that may be it's real name, because once when I was at Oxford looking at the races with my cousin Tom I heard quite a common woman say to another "There, Sarah, doesn't that make your pussy pout?" And then I saw that one of the rowing men's trousers were all split and those things were showing between his legs; and it looked most extraordinary. I couldn't quite see enough, but the more I looked the more I felt—well, the more I felt my pussy pouting, as the woman had said. So now I call ours pussies and their bow-wows, and my theory is that people have children when their bow-wows and pussies pout at the same time. Do you think that's it? Of course I can't imagine how it can possibly work, and I daresay I'm altogether wrong and it's really got something to do with W.C.'s.

Lord Folliot is coming to dinner, so I must go and dress. I'm sure he's a much worse bore than General Marchmont. He always will chuck me under the chin as though I was twelve. I hope you're write

again and tell me what you think about the pussies,
the bow-wows, and the Mapletons. I promise you I
won't show your letter to any one—even to Simpson—or Henry.

Your loving
Ermyntrude

P.S. What do you think castration means?

III

My dearest Ermyntrude,

There's such a fuss going on here with everyone getting ready for a picnic which we're all going
to that its almost impossible to write, and so you
must forgive me if I only write nonsense. As I know
all this evening will be taken up with a new kind of
billiards the General has taught us and that's all the
rage here at the present moment, I thought I'd better
seize this opportunity just to tell you, my dearest
darling Ermyntrude, how delightful it was to get
your perfectly sweet letter, and how I only wish I
could write one half as amusingly and cleverly and
altogether exquisitely as you. What you say about
babies I quite agree with, though I had never thought
of it until you said it, but there is one thing that I
still don't understand and that is what being in love
has to do with it all—I mean with having babies—
because, from what they always say in novels, it
seems to have a great deal. But with all this hulla-
baloo in the room I can't explain properly, and shall
put it off for another time, and only now tell you
that I asked Godfrey about that difficult word in
your P.S.—if he knew what it meant—after I'd made
him swear the most solemn secrecy, of course. But
first I must tell you that you are right, and he is the

one who's a year younger than me, and you are also right about his being like me, though it's conceited of me to say so, because every one says he's such a handsome boy. Well, about that word—and what do you think?—when I asked him, the wretch wouldn't do anything but burst out roaring with laughter and I couldn't get any answer out of him at all, except "Oh, Esmie, you really are too funny," which he said about half a dozen times, and then ran out of the room. I expect he went straight off and told Mr. Mapleton, and if he did I think it's abominable, after the secrecy he swore. But I suppose it only means that that word stands for something tremendously improper, and I shouldn't be at all surprised if it meant some kind of divorce.

By-the-bye, you are quite wrong about Mr. Mapleton. I am not in love with him at all. He is just an ordinary young man—nothing in the least particular. But I'll tell you what I rather suspect. I believe he's a little in love with me! Why I think so is that he doesn't seem at all anxious to be where I am, but keeps going out—either by himself or with Godfrey —for long walks and fishing expeditions, as if he wants to avoid me. Don't you think that's rather a sign? He sees I'm not in love with him, and so, in his disappointment, he tries to be with me as little as possible. Well, we shall see. I should like to write pages and pages about the Dean, and explain how completely wrong you are about him too, but I shall have to stop to help to do up the things. No, no, *no*,!

27

He is *most* beautiful. You should have seen him last Sunday in church, reading the lessons! He looked quite like a Saint, with the light from the stained glass window coming on to his face, and his voice was perfect. How heavenly he must be in his Cathedral, in a surplice, among all the little choirboys! Oh! I'm sure you'ld adore him as much as I do, if you could only see him, and perhaps you really *do*, and you're just pretending not to, to tease me.

As for the General, he's not nearly as bad as I expected.

Your loving
Esmeralda

IV

My dearest Esmeralda,

I went into the library this morning when my father was out, and got down the English Dictionary, to find out about Castration. The result wasn't very successful. First of all I could only find something about "having turrets and battlements like a castle," but then I discovered that I'd got hold of the wrong word—castellation, which I shouldn't think was at all the same thing. When I did find the right one, it simply said,—"Castrate; to emasculate, to geld," which didn't help much and when I found emasculate, it only said "to castrate, to geld," and as I was just finding geld, I heard someone coming into the room and had to put the book back as quickly as possible, as I didn't want my father to begin asking questions. However, it turned out to be only Henry with some coals, so I might have gone on after all, only then Simpson began calling me, and off I had to march for the promenade.

So you see the Dictionary hasn't been any more use than that mischievous Godfrey. I don't consider that you describe him very well. It's difficult to imagine a boy like you, and you don't tell me any details. For instance, are his teeth good? And are his shoulders broad? And his ears; do they stick out?—

but I don't suppose they can or he wouldn't be called handsome. If they don't, please pinch one of them from me, as a punishment for his bad behaviour.

Lord Folliot has given me a kitten, I don't like animals particularly, but I suppose I shall have to keep it, and Simpson promises to look after it for me. The horrid old man asked me what I was going to call it, and I said I thought that Pussy would do very well. I don't know what he thought of that,— and I don't care either. By-the-bye, my new theory is that being in love is merely a more polite way of saying that your pussy's pouting. What else can it mean? Won't you ask Mr. Mapleton if his bow-wow pouts for you, and won't you tell me in your next letter if your pussy pouts for the Dean?

For a wonder, I'm sitting in the drawing-room, as Simpson has gone out to one of her Congregationalist Meetings, and Mama is away, so I have the whole place to myself. In a minute Henry will come in to draw the curtains, and I shall give him this letter to post, so good-bye.

Your loving
Ermyntrude

P.S. It wasn't Henry after all, but Jessop, the butler, whom I hate.

V

My dearest Ermyntrude,

      Such a very extraordinary thing has just happened, and I must write and tell you at once, as I'm dying to know what you will think about it. I can't understand it at all. It's about Mr. Mapleton—that is, partly—do you remember that I said I thought he was in love with me because he avoided me so? Well, now I don't think that can be it, but I had better begin at the beginning and then you can judge. I was sitting in the verandah after tea this evening, trying to get through my Canto of Dante—did I tell you that I was doing it with the Dean? It was he who suggested it, and he's been so wonderfully kind about it, and oh, my dearest Ermyntrude, what a beautiful poem it is—though I must say I think I like Tennyson better. Well, there I was, quite alone for a wonder, until it began to get cold and I thought I'd go indoors, so I was going in by the Morning Room window, which was wide open, and I did just get inside, but then I was surprised by hearing somebody talking, which was quite surprising because hardly any one ever uses the Morning Room—especially at that time in the day. I thought it was rather funny, and then I suddenly recognized that it was Mr. Mapleton's voice that was talking, but not at all his usual voice, and it was all quite dark—much darker than outside—and so altogether I was so surprised that I stood quite still and couldn't help listening. And what do you think I heard? You'll never guess—only I only half heard it really, because it was so mumbling and indistinct and it seemed so funny and extraordinary. I'm sure he was making love. He kept on saying "I love you more than anybody in the world," and things like that, and "Do you love me? Do you—love me as much as I love you?" a great many times, and "You're the most beautiful creature in the world, how can you be so beautiful?" and "My dearest dearest dearest angel," and things like that. Don't you think he must have been making love? Of course I couldn't imagine who he was talking to, but I thought it might be the under housemaid, who's quite pretty, but not the most beautiful person in the world—but then people always do exaggerate when they're making love don't they—and then I was just wondering whether perhaps it was Carrie, when somebody else said "Darling—darling"—just like that, and my dear, it was Godfrey! That gave me such a jump that I very nearly dropped all my books—the grammar and dictionary and everything—but I luckily didn't, and by that time the room seemed rather lighter and I made out that Godfrey's voice must have come from behind a screen there is going across, so I stretched out as far as I could, and just managed to see round the screen to the sofa. And Mr. Mapleton was there too,

with his arm round Godfrey's neck, and they were kissing and their hair was all tousled, but the most extraordinary thing of all was that their buttons were so much undone that their shirts were all coming out. Wasn't it too peculiar for words? But just then someone began to come along the passage outside, and they jumped up very quickly, and Mr. Mapleton began walking towards the window, so I slipped out and ran round by the front door. I expect it was the maid coming to shut the window. I haven't said anything about it to either of them yet. I'm not sure whether I shall—even to Godfrey. They might think I'd been listening on purpose, which I wasn't at all. They seemed quite as usual at dinner, and now here I am writing to you as fast as I can—I'm so excited and somehow rather frightened too—I don't know why. At least I was frightened when I looked round the screen. Do you think—my dear, do you think it's possible for them to be in love? I'm almost sure they must be, but then if they are, I can't understand at all, because how can they have babies? Do answer by return of post, I beg and implore you.

Your loving
Esmeralda

VI

Dearest Esmeralda,

What a lark! I'm in a hurry, as Mama for a wonder is taking me out to some dreadful tea party this afternoon, but I must write a few words now, as you ask me to. And so that's what you call nothing ever happening, is it? I only wish anything half as amusing would happen here. No such luck. But I don't think you've made the most of your opportunities. It was a great chance for finding out some interesting things. For instance, you don't say which buttons were undone. Was it too dark to see? I don't believe it was, but you were too flurried, and didn't look properly. I'm sure I should have, if it had been me. I really think you ought to try and discover some more from Godfrey. Couldn't you lead the conversation round to bow-wows—in quite a general way? I wish I could talk to him for a little. It might be easier for him to tell things to someone who wasn't his sister. I suppose, as you say, two bow-wows can't have babies, but I can't see why on earth they shouldn't pout at one another. The great question is—how do they pout? I command you to ask him. You can ask him from me, if you like. Do you know, when I read your letter, I began to wish that I *was* Godfrey—I suppose because then I should know all about it. But I must stop and go and dress. I'll write again soon.

Your loving
Ermyntrude

P.S. No. I'm not sure. I think on the whole I'd rather have been Mr. Mapleton.

VII

Dearest Ermyntrude,

There has been the most awful row. Papa went in by accident yesterday morning to get a shoe-horn, and found Mr. Mapleton in Godfrey's bed. He was most fearfully angry, told Mr. Mapleton that he would have to go away out of England and live abroad for ever and ever, or he would have him put in prison, and stormed at Godfrey like anything, and said he would flog him, only he was too old to be flogged, but he *ought* to be flogged, and that he had disgraced himself and his family, and that it could never be wiped out, never, and that he couldn't hold up his head again with such a son, and that as Godfrey wasn't to be flogged he would have to be punished in some even worse way,—but none of us know what yet. It was too dreadful for words. Godfrey told me all about it. Mr. Mapleton went away that very morning, immediately after breakfast, but he didn't come down to it, so perhaps he didn't have any, and Mama has been almost in tears ever since, and Papa has hardly spoken to anyone. The Dean has been looking very grave. I don't know what would have happened if it hadn't been for General Marchmont, who got up a croquet tournament yesterday, which put us into better spirits, as we had to make the arrangements about it, it is to be the American kind—everyone will play every one else, and the one who wins most games will get a prize from the General. Papa said that Godfrey wasn't to join, as he wasn't fit to associate with the others, which is a great pity. Poor Godfrey is in such dreadful disgrace, and I am very sorry for him. I suppose it was a frightfully wicked thing to do, but the curious thing is he doesn't seem at all wicked, and I really do believe I'm fonder of him than I've ever been before. I talked to him for quite a long time yesterday before dinner. I went into the morning room, and he was there, so I began to say how sorry I was. But before I'd said very much he turned round and walked towards the window, and then I saw that he was crying. I hardly knew what to do, so I went on talking for a little, and at last I threw my arms round his neck and kissed him a great many times, which seemed to comfort him although he began to cry harder than ever at first. But in the end he told me all about Mr. Mapleton, and how fond he was of him, and how unhappy he was to think he'd never see him again, and when I asked him whether he was in love with him, he said yes, he was, and why not?—that he loved him better than anyone in the world and always would as long as he lived, and then he began crying again. And he said he did not think he'd done anything wicked at all, and it seems the Greeks used to do it too,—at least the Athenians, who were the best of the Greeks—

42

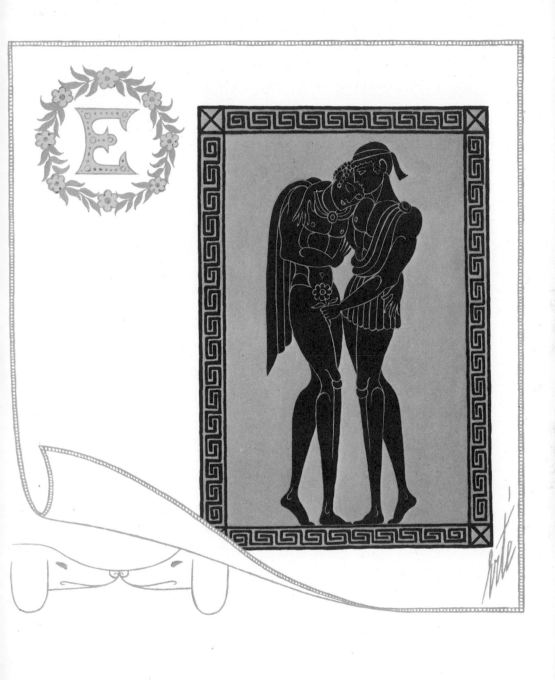

which is very funny, don't you think? And he said that Mr. Mapleton agreed with everything he'd said, and in fact he had told him most of it, and as for Papa he said he was a silly old man and he expected he'd done just the same himself when he was a boy at school but that he'd forgotten all about it. Of course I wouldn't let him say things against Papa, but really it seems very extraordinary if what Godfrey says is true, and I can't make it out at all, can you? I've made up my mind what to do, though, I'm going to ask the Dean to explain it to me. Isn't that a good idea? He's so wise he must know everything, and he's so good and kind that I'm sure he wouldn't get angry, as I'm certain Papa would if I said anything about it to *him*. I'm waiting for a good opportunity to find the Dean by himself, but at present it's rather difficult because there always seems to be somebody who insists upon playing off their game of croquet with me. When I've got it out of him I'll let you know. But dearest Ermyntrude, do write and tell me what *you* think, I believe you're almost as clever as the Dean.

Your loving
Esmeralda

P.S. Godfrey has just told me that he is to be taken away from school, and sent abroad too, as well as Mr. Mapleton, but of course not to the same place and only for a year, but Godfrey says he hates the thought of it.

P.P.S. I forgot to say that when I was talking to Godfrey I tried several times to ask him your question but somehow or other I couldn't get it in. I find that there are some things it's very difficult indeed to talk about, just when one wants to most.

VIII

My dearest Esmeralda,

Your letters get more and more exciting, and make me more and more envious. Here am I as usual in the drawing-room, by the fire, all alone, except for the kitten curled up in its basket, and I feel as if I'd been here for the last five hundred years. I've taken to sitting in this gaunt room lately because it's a good way of escaping from Simpson, and as Mama's again away there's no fear of visitors. It's true that Lord Folliot came yesterday, but I don't think he'll come again. I don't like him at all. He first chucked me under the chin, and then put his hand (which was more like a claw) on my chest, and asked me how Pussy was doing. He winked and grinned and was quite ridiculous—all wrinkled and horrid. I'm quite sure his bow-wow was pouting as hard as it could all the time. I thought to myself "Why should *your* bow-wow be allowed to pout as it likes, you disgusting old man, and poor Godfrey, when *his* does, get into such hot water? It really is a great shame. You must give Godfrey my love, though I think if he'd cried rather less I should like him better. Of course it would have been different if he had been really whipped. Would it have been with a birch rod? I was as nasty as I could be to

Lord Folliot, and he went away looking sillier than ever. I expect it'll make you angry, but I can't help thinking he's rather like the Dean. I wonder if you've had your conversation with him yet. It will be great fun when you do, but if I were you I shouldn't believe a word he said. Clergymen always tell stories.

Talking of conversations, it's rather amusing, I had one the other day with who do you think?—Henry! He nearly always comes after tea to take the things away, so I thought it would be rather amusing to talk to him. I think I told you about the butler, Jessop, and how I dislike him. He's got very thin lips, that he keeps pressed together very close, and he stands up very straight and looks most severe. I had a quarrel with him a long time ago, when I was quite small. I used to go down to the Servant's Hall, and they all used to pet me a great deal, and sometimes they kissed me; but one day Jessop began kissing me more than I wanted, so I made him stop, and ever since I believe he's hated me; and I'm sure I've hated him. So I thought I'd find out what Henry thought of him, and as he was clearing away the tea I said, just to begin "Is Jessop out today?" He said he was, so I said, "Does he go out often?"—"Pretty often, Miss"—"Does he make you work very hard"—"Oh yes, Miss"—"He's very strict, I suppose?" "Oh, he's that strict, Miss!"—"You don't like him much, then?"—"No, Miss, nothing particklar—not as you might say, anything out of the common,—not as I like some." Then he

48

went on putting the cups on to the tray. I thought it was very nice of him to be so easy to talk to, so I began to laugh and said "And who *do* you like?" "Do you like Mrs. Codrington" (She's the cook)— "Yes, Miss, I like Mrs. Codrington". I saw that he was smiling, and then while he was making a clatter with the cups he said something else that was really rather extraordinary, and in a very low voice—"And I like *you*, Miss." I could hardly hear it, but I'm certain he did say it, though I pretended not to have noticed anything and took up a book. He went out very quickly after that, and neither of us has said anything about it since, though we have had a few more conversations. Here he is. I must stop, as I shall have to give him this letter to post. Please give me a full account of what you got out of the Dean, and I insist upon your asking him every question that comes into your head.

Your loving
Ermyntrude

P.S. Something so curious has happened that I've opened this again to tell you about it. When I was giving this letter to Henry to post, I dropped it, and we both put down our hands to pick it up. Somehow or other he took hold of my fingers instead of the letter. I felt rather awkward, but just then the kitten took it into its head to jump out of its basket, so I ran after it and put it back. While I was doing that he went and drew the curtains, and then he went out, without taking the letter, which was still on the floor. He didn't say anything at all, and nor did I. Now I've rung the bell, and I shall put this into a new envelope and give it him again, and try not to drop it this time. He'll be here in a moment. It's rather odd. His fingers seemed very astrong.

IX

My dearest Ermyntrude,

I've got something very surprising to tell you, and when it happened it surprised me just as much. Have you noticed how funny it is, the way things always seem to turn out quite differently from what you expected? Why is it, do you think? I always try and imagine as hard as I can what's going to happen beforehand, don't you?—but when it does happen, it's somehow or other always something else—only I expect you're so horribly clever you can always imagine right. But I wonder whether even you would have guessed about my conversation with the Dean, and that it would have ended by—but I must tell you first that I found him alone in the study this morning, as I hoped I would, as Papa had gone out with the Agent, and as it was such a good opportunity I said to myself that I mustn't miss it, because it was just the time to ask him about Godfrey and Mr. Mapleton. So I did, but what a wicked teasing creature you are, to say that the Dean is like Lord Folliot! Of course he isn't at all, but as I'm sure you're only laughing at me all the time, I won't pay any attention. Well, I thought I'd better begin in rather a roundabout way, so I asked him about Dante, and Beatrice, and he said the most beautiful

51

things about them that you can imagine, and then I said I supposed Dante was in love with Beatrice and he seemed very pleased and even more polite than ever, and said more and more beautiful things, and was far more poetical than I'm sure Lord Folliot could ever be. When I asked whether it wasn't wrong to be in love, and he moved his chair nearer and said "My dear Miss Esmeralda, surely you cannot think that!" and said that love was the purification and the sanctification of something that I can't remember now, but it was all very nice, and at last he took hold of my hand, so I thought the moment had come and said "then why was Papa so angry with Godfrey?" Directly I'd said it I saw that it couldn't have been the right moment, because he got very startled indeed, and dropped my hand, and asked me in quite a stiff voice how I could ask such a question. But I was determined this time not to be afraid, and so I said that Godfrey was in love with Mr. Mapleton, and if it was not wrong to be in love, why shouldn't he be? He seemed terribly shocked, and threw up his hands, and said "Love! Love for that perverse, misguided, unhappy young man! What a profanation, my dear young lady, what a profanation!" But I said Godfrey himself had told me so, and then he said that Godfrey was very wicked and that I shouldn't listen to what he said. So then I remembered some of the things that Godfrey had told me about the Greeks, so I asked if *they* had all been very wicked, and whether Socrates hadn't been a very good man, and whether he hadn't been in love with young men —and perhaps very like Mr. Mapleton? He said that I was touching upon a most painful subject, that it was one of the mysteries of Providence that the highest and the lowest sometimes met in the same person, and that the Greeks had not had the benefit of the teaching of Our Lord, which I suppose is quite true. Then I remembered something else that Godfrey had said, so I asked him whether he hadn't very likely felt just the same as Godfrey when he was at school himself, and when I said that, he got up and walked up and down the room, and seemed quite agitated. So I thought I must be right, and then I had a sudden idea, and said it almost without thinking, directly it came into my head—"Oh, Dr. Bartlett, I believe you were in love with Papa!" You see I knew they had been at school together, and do you know I really believe it was true because he got very red and came up to me and said in a low voice "No, no, Miss Esmeralda, let me beg you to put such distressing thoughts out of your mind. These subjects are not fit for a pure young girl to dwell upon. They come as a temptation—a terrible temptation. Turn away from them I beseech you—fly from them as you would from the Evil One himself. Let me counsel you, let me help you, let me guide your thoughts towards"—but I can't remember what it was exactly he wanted to guide my thoughts towards, except that he went on talking for a very long time, and then suddenly I found to my great

surprise what I'm sure you couldn't possibly have guessed—he was making love to me, and asking me to marry him, and had gone down on his knees beside my chair, so that I didn't at all know what to do, especially as I very nearly burst out laughing, because he did look so very extraordinary. But just then I heard General Marchmont's voice out of the window, calling me, so I jumped up and said I must go and play a game of croquet. He seemed very distressed and asked me whether I wouldn't answer him. I said I would this evening, and that's all. It's a dreadful nuisance, but I suppose I shall have to. Of course I'm very fond of him and admire him I'm sure more than almost everyone else in the world, but what surprised me most of all was that when he asked me to marry him, although I'd always thought it would be the most wonderful thing that could possibly happen to me, I didn't want to a bit. I don't understood it in the least, unless it is that perhaps I —but I shan't tell you any more just now—so there!

Your loving
Esmeralda

P.S. Have you had any more conversations with Henry?

X

Dearest Esmeralda,

I ought to have answered your last letter some days ago. I can't write much now, as I am rather hurried. I was very glad that you didn't say that you would marry the horrid old Dean. It would have been very nasty. I think I can guess why it was that you didn't, because I'm sure that if your pussy had pouted it would have been quite different. I agree with you about it's being very difficult to know what's going to happen, but I think as I don't imagine what it's going to be so much as you do, I'm less surprised. The funny thing is that you learn a lot anyhow—whether you're surprised or not. But I must stop now.

Your loving
Ermyntrude

P.S. I have had some more conversations with Henry.

XI

My dearest Ermyntrude,

It's abominable of me not to have written before, but really I've had hardly any time to spare, there have been so many things going on, and it's all been such fun, but not the sort of things you can write about. And even now I've only got one minute, just to send you my love, my dearest Ermyntrude, and to say that I'm feeling very excited because it is the Swinford's dance tonight, and I'm going, and so is Tony and Amabel and Mama, and in fact everybody including General Marchmont. Won't it be delightful? Do you think anything very specially amusing and charming will happen? I wonder and wonder, but I can never make up my mind, because there are so many other things to think about. I've been in a great fright about my dress not being done in time, but it has been, so that's one blessing, and I've promised two dances to General Marchmont. I don't think I ever told you that the Dean had gone away—he went the very next morning after I'd told him that I didn't want to marry him. So he won't be at the dance, but perhaps he wouldn't have been anyway, as I don't believe clergymen usually go to dances. I can't write any more, Carrie is calling me. If anything special does happen at the dance, I'll let you know all about it as soon as I can.

Your most loving
Esmeralda

XII

My dearest Esmeralda,

  As I've got some spare time to write to you in, I'd better begin at once. I expect this will be rather a long letter, but though I thought I wouldn't at first, I've made up my mind to tell you everything that's happened, so that can't be helped. There's just been a fearful rumpus here. I'd better tell you that it all began about a fortnight ago, that time I told you about, when I dropped the letter. It was then that my pussy began to pout. I daresay that you will think it very shocking that it should pout for a footman. But Henry was not like an ordinary footman. He was much better-looking and taller and stronger. He had very black hair that was rather curly, and black eyebrows and dark blue eyes and a straight nose that turned up at the end which made him look impudent, and a small mouth with perfectly white teeth, and a very nice neck indeed. I'm sure if you could have seen him in his dark green livery and silver buttons your pussy would have pouted too,—especially if you could have felt what his fingers were like. I didn't tell you, but that time I wanted to hug him, and I really think I might have, if the kitten hadn't jumped out of its basket just at that instant. Wasn't it an absurd joke that

61

the two pussies should have begun playing pranks at the same time? Then when I rang the bell it was Jessop who came up. Henry told me afterwards he was too frightened to, and pretended to be ill. The next day Simpson would insist upon my playing duets with her the whole evening, so there was no opportunity for saying anything to Henry when he took away the tea. But the day after that Simpson went out, so I went down to the drawing-room as usual, and then it was most tiresome because Jessop came and did everything, and I thought Henry must have gone out for the evening. But at half past six he came in when I wasn't at all expecting him. He said that a window was broken in the backstairs and that Jessop was out and that my father was out, and would I give the order to have it mended, as last time my father had been very angry at orders being given without his leave. So I said yes, and then he said, "It's near the top of the backstairs, Miss," and didn't go away. So I said, "Is it a large pane?" And he said "Not very, Miss, would you like to see it?" So I said "You'd better show it me." I was rather frightened when I said that, but he answered very quickly "Yes, Miss, I think that would be the best way." And then he said we'd better have a candle, because it was "that dark on them stairs," so he lighted one, and off we went—upstairs, and then round along the little landing under the dome, and then through the door to the backstairs, and down them until we came to the window with the broken

62

pane. Henry held up the candle to show it me, and said "You see, Miss, it ain't a very big hole." I leant over to look at it better, and put my head too near the candle and my hair gave a frizzle, which gave Henry a fright, and he said, "Oh, take care, Miss! Your hair!" I said "Would you mind if I burnt my hair, Henry?" And he said "Mind Miss? Why they might take both my ears off me, that they might, Miss, before I left any manner of harm come to your hair." So I laughed, and said "That would be a pity, Henry; you've got such nice ears."—"Not as nice as your hair, Miss."—"Why do you like my hair so much Henry?"—"It's got a colour on it the same as the butter down in our country, Miss—Dorsetshire, that is"—"Do you think it feels as nice as it looks, Henry?"—"That I do, Miss!"—So I laughed again, just a little, and said "Then why don't you stroke it?" And then he didn't say anything, but put out his hand, and looked at my eyes, and I looked at his eyes, and then—well, it didn't seem to be me any longer, but it was like something else that made me do things, and I put my arms round his neck all of a sudden, and he hugged me so hard that I could only just breathe, and it felt as if he was hugging me with the whole of his body. And then the candle fell over and went out, and it was pitch dark, and after that I hardly know what happened, because it was so very exciting, but somehow I began to half lie down on the stairs, which are quite steep and nothing but wood, and Henry was on the top of me,

63

hugging me just as much as ever, so you can imagine that it wasn't particularly comfortable. I forgot to say that directly he hugged me I felt my pussy pouting so enormously that I didn't know what to do— except hug him back, which seemed only to make it pout more. But when we were lying down it did it even more still. Then Henry began pulling up my skirt and even my petticoat, and I began helping him, and it was very funny—we were both in such a hurry, and his body twisted about so much and he breathed so hard that I half began to feel frightened. But he held me too tightly for me to have possibly got away, even if I'd wanted to, and then suddenly my all of a sudden my pussy began to hurt most horribly, and I very nearly screamed. It was as if something was going right through me, but though it hurt my pussy so, it made it stop pouting at the same time and begin to purr instead, as if it liked it, and I think it did like it better than anything else in the world. I can't understand why pussies should like so much being hurt. And the curious thing was that I suppose I liked it too, because I went on kissing Henry more and more, and although I was so uncomfortable and hot and all squashed-up and disarranged and I believe nearly crying, I didn't at all want it to stop, and I was very sorry when Henry said he would have to go and lay the dinner or Jessop would ask him where he'd been.

I must tell you that Henry told me afterwards that what he'd said about Papa and the orders for the window was a story, and he'd said it to try and make me go there with him, and if I hadn't, he told me that he'd settled to give warning and go away that very night. He said that his bow-wow had begun to pout so much, especially when he was handing me the vegetables, that he couldn't have stood it any longer. But that night, when he handed me the vegetables, it was a great lark, because my pussy was pouting, too. After dinner, when I'd gone up to bed, it was still more of a lark. I'd arranged it with Henry. When all the lights were out I opened my door a very little, and then he came in, and after we'd kissed each other a great deal we took off our clothes. I was very excited to see what his bow-wow was like, but I was astonished to see that he hadn't got one, but a very funny big pink thing standing straight up instead. I was rather frightened, because I thought he might be deformed, which wouldn't have been at all nice, so I asked him what it was. Then he laughed so much that I thought every one would hear, and at last I discovered that it *was* his bow-wow after all, and it turns out that that is what they get like when they pout! I was very pleased indeed, and so was my pussy when his bow-wow went into it, and after that we went to bed. Ever since then he's come every night, and I've enjoyed myself very much. It's a pity I didn't know about it before, because we might have begun doing it directly he came here, and I might have done it before that with the last George but one, who looked quite pretty, but of course not nearly so handsome as Henry.

We had great fun in the day time too. At first we were pretty frightened of being caught but we got less and less frightened, and I suppose we were rather foolish, because—well, we were found out, but in rather an extraordinary way, so I'll tell you how it all happened. I was sitting in the schoolroom yesterday by myself, as Simpson was out as usual, and someone came in. I thought it would be Henry, but it was Jessop, and he said he wanted to speak to me. I said he might, and then he looked very severe, and said, "I wonder you're not ashamed of yourself, Miss Ermie." I asked him way, and he said, "Oh, you know well enough, Miss Ermie—carrying on something awful with Henry." Of course I said I didn't know what he was talking about, but he only got more severe, and pressed his horrid thin lips closer together, and said "It's not a bit of use you're playing the innocent. I'm bound to go straight to Sir William this moment, and tell him what I know." I did get very frightened then, because of course I knew there'ld be frightful ructions if my father heard of it, and I didn't know what to do. So I thought the best plan was to be as nice as possible to Jessop, and try and persuade him not to tell. But at first it didn't seem any good, because he went on being very cross—"Now none of your wheedling with *me* Miss Ermie; you know quite well it's my

67

duty to go to Sir William"—and so on. But I went on begging him more and more, and then all of a sudden he changed altogether and said in quite a soft voice—"You're nice enough to me now, when you want to get something out of me. As soon as you get it, it'ld be a different tune." I said I should always be very grateful indeed, but he said "No, Miss, you wouldn't. You don't like me, that's what it is. You don't care for me two pins." Then I thought I'd better tell a great fib, so I said I liked him very much. And he said "Like me? Like me, do you? Do you like me as much as Henry? That's what I'm wondering." I said I liked him in a different way, and then he came much closer to me, and turned all white, and said, very low indeed, "But I want the same way. Do you understand that, Miss Ermie? That's the way you've got to like me. You like Henry and you like me. Well then you've got to like both or neither. That's what it is. And now shall I go to Sir William?" Then I understood what he was up to, and I felt cold all over, but I didn't see any way out of it, so in the end I agreed. I said he might come that night instead of Henry to my bed room, and he was going away, when he turned round and said "No, Miss Ermie, I don't trust you. You'll get out of it. Now, now!" And then he ran at me and kissed me very violently indeed, and seemed much more excited even then Henry. And though at first I didn't like it at all, afterwards I didn't mind it so much. But in the middle of it I heard a scream, and I couldn't think what had happened, and Jessop went out of the room very quickly, and there was Simpson in a faint on the floor. She'd seen Jessop with his bow-wow in my pussy, and that was why she'd fainted. When she came to she hardly said anything, and I was surprised that she didn't rush off and tell everybody all about it. Instead of that she said she was too ill to come down to dinner. Jessop didn't dare to come to my bedroom afterwards, but Henry did. Just as we were beginning to enjoy ourselves, there was a knock at the door. Henry hid himself under the bed, and then the old Simpson came in in her dressing gown. She began embracing me and talking a great deal in a whining tone of voice. She said I was her dearest child, and that I had fallen and how terrible it was and what would Mama say, and all sorts of rubbish, and all the time she was kissing me, and calling me her dearest darling Ermie, and saying how much she loved me, till I got very bored, and wouldn't think what it was all coming to. But what do you think it was? She was the same as Jessop. She wanted to get into bed with me, and she said that if I'ld let her do that she'd never never tell. It was really very absurd. I don't know why, but I'd never thought before that one pussy might pout for another, but of course if bow-wows pout for one another there's no reason why pussies shouldn't too. So there was Simpson's pussy pouting for mine; but I wouldn't have it. I think you must draw the line somewhere, especially if Henry's

under the bed, and I drew it at Simpson's pussy. I told her to go away, and that she might tell everybody anything she liked, and that I never wanted to see her again. And as she was going I said something else, that I'd heard Henry say about Jessop— "And God rot you, Simpson, into the bargain," which shocked her a good deal, because she turned round in the doorway and said "Oh, Ermie, Ermie! As well as all the rest—bad language!" And then she went, and Henry came out from under the bed.

All this happened last night when you were at your dance, having a gay time I suppose with General Marchmont. But we had an even gayer time here this morning, when the old woman went and had hysterics in the library, and told my father about me and Jessop. Jessop was sent for, and denied it, and said it was Henry, and Henry was sent for and said it was Jessop, and I was sent for and wouldn't say anything at all. It would be no use describing the rest of the row, which was very silly, and just like other rows, only worse, but they were all three dismissed, including Simpson, for not looking after me enough, and going too often to the Congregational Meetings. I'd always suspected that she used to go there for the sake of some bouncing bow-wow, but now I think it must have been for a mewing pussy, but anyhow that's the end of *her*. As for me I'm to be sent off to Germany with a German governess Mama has discovered, almost at once. She's the daughter of a pastor in some dismal town in Saxony

71

—Schmettau or something—and there I'm to stay. It doesn't sound exciting, and I'm afraid I shall miss Henry a good deal. I found a little note from him on a crumpled-up piece of paper on my dressing-table this evening. I suppose he'd got one of the maids to put it there. It said "Good-bye Miss. They won't let me stay here no longer. They want me to go to Canada, but I'd run away first. Oh, Miss, when shall I see you again? Yours respectfully, Henry." I forgot to say that he always went on calling me Miss, even when he was hugging me most, which I liked very much. And really on the whole I'm not sorry that any of it's happened, because, although the row has been a nuisance, I know a great many things now that I didn't know before.

When I've got the address in Germany I'll send it you, and I hope you'll write to me there. Perhaps I'll have a letter from you tomorrow morning describing the dance. Now good-bye, I am rather tired.

Your loving
Ermyntrude

XIII

My dearest darling beloved Ermyntrude,

It has all happened as I most wished, and I am going to marry General Marchmont! He asked me to last night at the dance, and I said Yes, and then—oh, my dear!—he kissed me! He is the kindest dearest bravest most wonderful man in the world, and though he is fifty I'm quite sure I could never love anybody one millionth as much as I love him. He's been in two wars, and I don't know how many battles, and has got a whole row of medals, and his regiment was the Rifle Brigade, which is one of the very best there is. He said that I should be his own beloved wife, and the mother of his children, and that he would teach me in the sphere of home and womanhood to grow up a perfect queen! Wasn't it too lovely? I wouldn't tell you before how fond of him I was because I thought you might laugh at me and think that I only cared for him as much as I cared for the Dean. But now it's all come right and I'm perfectly happy, only I want to have some babies as quickly as I can. I never thought all the time we were wondering about being in love and having babies that I should know all about it so soon. But I must stop and go and find Edward—that is his

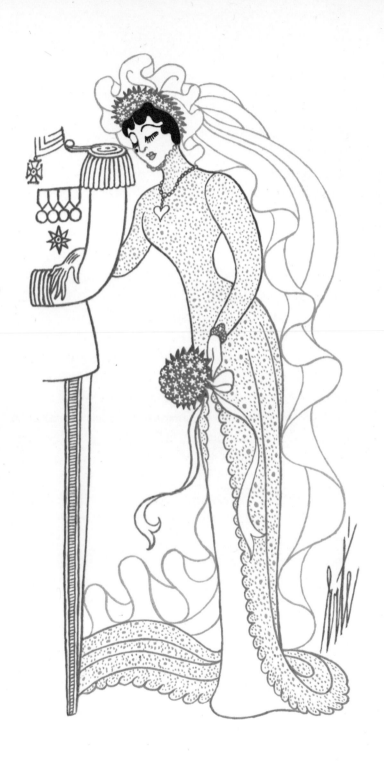

name! Isn't it exquisite! I shall write to you again directly I know when we are to be married.

Your own very most loving
Esmeralda

P.S. I forgot to say that I had a letter from Godfrey the other day. He is in a Saxon town in Germany, called Schmettau. He lives with the schoolmaster, and he says it's not very exciting, but as the Parson lives next door it ought to be good for him.— Oh my dear! Edward has just come in, and we are to be married in September! Isn't it too exciting for words? And he wants me to say that he hopes you will be my bridesmaid.